CLAUDE

Going for Gold

ALEX T. SMITH

Claude is a dog.
Claude is a small dog.
Claude is a small, plump dog
who wears a lovely red jumper
and a very fetching beret.

very fetching
beret

lovely red
jumper

He lives at 112 Waggy Avenue
with Mr and Mrs Shinyshoes and
his best friend Sir Bobblysock.

This is Sir Bobblysock.

Every day, after Mr and Mrs Shinyshoes have cried, 'Toodle-pip, Claude!' and left for work, Claude and Sir Bobblysock go on an adventure.

Where
will
they
go
today?

It was a Tuesday and, for once, Sir Bobblysock couldn't wait to get out of the house.

Claude, you see, had woken up with ants in his pants. Not REAL ones, of course (that had been yesterday's excitement). He simply couldn't sit still!

He ate his breakfast with his bottom waggling about.

He brushed his teeth hopping on one leg.

And putting his beret on took approximately 45 minutes because he had to pretend that it was first a pancake, and then a flying saucer whizzing through space. (A flying saucer that knocked over two packets of cereal and an entire jug of milk.)

Eventually, however, the two chums made it out of the front door.

Claude took a big sniff.

Today smelt of...

112

'ADVENTURE!' he said in his
Outdoor Voice (because he was
outdoors).

'LET'S GO AND FIND
SOMETHING EXCITING
TO DO!'

Sir Bobblysock was more
interested in finding a frothy
coffee and somewhere to park
himself for a quiet moment, but he
nodded his head in agreement.

And so the two friends bustled
along Waggy Avenue.

Claude looked
for an adventure
everywhere.

Mr Lovelybuns was installing a
lovely big cream horn in his front
window, but that didn't get
Claude's eyebrows waggling this
morning. His tummy was still full
from breakfast.

Belinda Hintova-Tint had an appointment book FULL of curly perms to be done today, but that didn't get Claude's bottom wiggling. (Besides, Claude had helped her last week and Sir Bobblysock was still recovering.)

At Miss Melon's fruit and veg shop there was usually a funny-shaped cucumber or some plums that needed juggling, but today there was nothing.

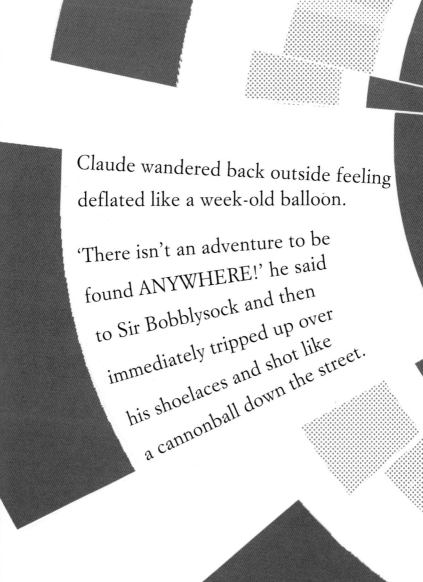

Claude wandered back outside feeling deflated like a week-old balloon.

'There isn't an adventure to be found ANYWHERE!' he said to Sir Bobblysock and then immediately tripped up over his shoelaces and shot like a cannonball down the street.

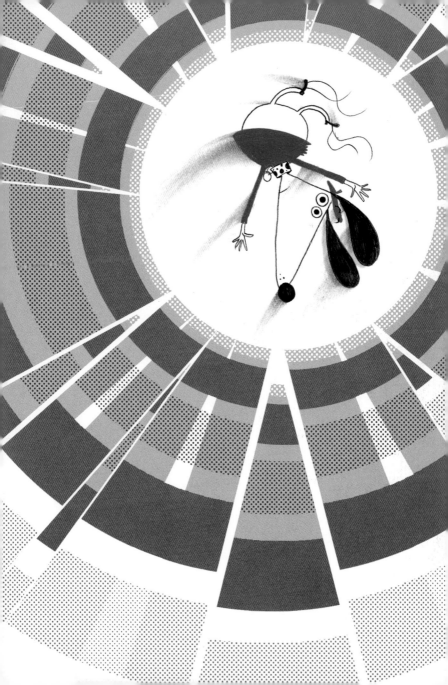

Sir Bobblysock had ever such a job to keep up with him! It wasn't easy to clatter downhill whilst and almost impossible trying to balance a large frothy coffee and a handful of Garibaldis at the same time...

16

Eventually Claude came to a stop by walloping into a marching band who were right at that very moment **oomp-pah-pah-ing** around the corner with quite a crowd behind them.

When Claude managed to sit
up, his head was spinning.
Everyone was looking at him,
so Claude looked back at them.

What a strange group
they were!

JANGLE!

In amongst the band and the crowd of spectators waving flags were a lot of very healthy looking people. They appeared to be wearing JUST their vests and some very snazzy, stretchy knickers.

Sir Bobblysock whipped on his specs to get a better look.

Claude was about to ask what was going on when a terribly hearty woman in a leotard bounded over...

'GOODNESS!' she cried.
'I've never seen ANYONE
move so fast!'

Claude smoothed
down his ears.

'My name is Ivanna Hurlit-Farr,'
she said, and she went on to explain
exactly what on earth was
happening.

Today was the day of the
STONKING BIG SPORTS DAY
where teams of people from all over
the place were getting together to
have a go at lots of sports. There
would be medals for all the winners
and a gigantic trophy too!

Ivanna wafted her hand in the direction of two chaps holding the most enormous glitzy gold cup you have ever seen, as well as a collection of little gold discs on snazzy red ribbons.

'Ooooooooooooh!'
went the crowd.

Claude had never seen anything so
sparkly, and Sir Bobblysock was
already thinking how lovely those
medals would look around his
neck. Especially if he wore them at
the captain's table on a cruise or at
a summer garden party.

'Can I join in please?' asked
Claude. This sounded like just
the sort of adventure he'd been
looking for!

Ivanna looked Claude up and
down. 'Do you have any sports
clothes? Any snazzy knickers?'

Well, Claude had a lot of things
in his beret, but he didn't think
he had any snazzy sports knickers.
He shook his head sadly.

26

'Never mind, I'm sure we can find you some!' said Ivanna encouragingly, lunging in her own.

Well, that sealed it! 'You're on the
team,' cried Ivanna, 'and this must
be your coach!'

She pointed at Sir Bobblysock who was still gazing at all the snazzy sports knickers and leotards around him.

Claude didn't like to say it was actually his best friend Sir Bobblysock, so he just nodded his head and the crowd shouted,

'HURRAH!'

Before they knew what was
happening, Claude and Sir
Bobblysock were up on Ivanna's
shoulders and everyone cheered
and **oomp-pah-pahed** their way
to the STONKING BIG
SPORTS DAY stadium.

It was only Sir Bobblysock who noticed two people who weren't cheering...

They were standing in the shadows
flipping coins and chewing on
toothpicks. Maybe they were on
a different team, he thought.

As the enormous gold cup and the medals marched past, they looked at each other and chuckled to themselves in a VERY naughty fashion.

Sir Bobblysock thought they too were imagining how nice that trophy would be on their knick-knack shelf at home.

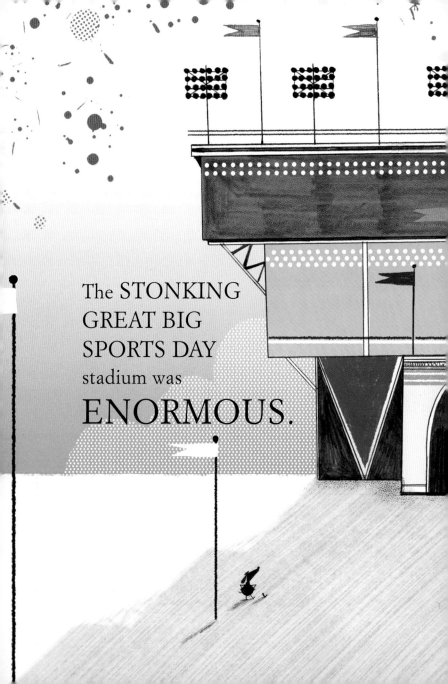

The STONKING
GREAT BIG
SPORTS DAY
stadium was
ENORMOUS.

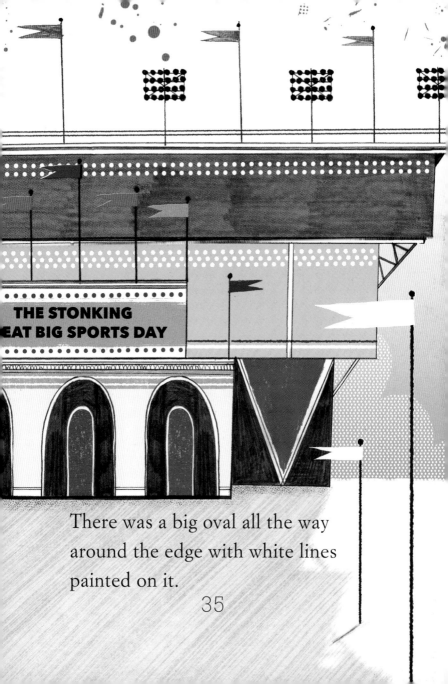

**THE STONKING
EAT BIG SPORTS DAY**

There was a big oval all the way
around the edge with white lines
painted on it.

In the middle was a gigantic lawn that Claude thought could have done with a few flowers planted on it, or at least a nice water feature or something, to jazz it all up a bit.

There was also a big building with a 'Swimming Pool' sign on it, and various other rooms where different sports were played.

Claude helped place the trophy and medals on a special podium in the middle of the stadium and everyone clapped – it was going to be an exciting afternoon!

38

Whilst the crowd took their
seats and the band popped their
trombones away, Ivanna Hurlit-Farr
eyeballed Claude. His jumper was
lovely, but not quite the ticket for
the day's events.

'Here are some sports knickers!'
she said heartily. 'Do you have a
vest you can wear with them?'

Well, of course, Claude did –
he always kept a vest in his
beret in case of sudden
draughts – so he wiggled into
that and put on the knickers.

They were gigantic!

'Oh dear…' said Ivanna.

'Don't worry!' cried Claude and he yanked them right up under his armpits. He wrapped the drawstring three times around his belly and finished it off with a nice bow.

Sir Bobblysock supervised from the side and told Claude that wearing his shorts like that would help to keep a chill off his kidneys.

Then Claude stashed his beret
down his vest and popped on a
sweatband.

Sir Bobblysock, wanting to get in the spirit of things now he was Claude's coach, put a whistle around his neck and popped a sweatband on too, even though he was dreadfully worried it would flatten his curly perm.

TOOT!
TOOT!

Gosh, did Claude and Sir
Bobblysock now look the part!

'LOVELY!' said Ivanna. 'Now
we are ready!'

Claude, Sir Bobblysock and all
their team mates cheered,
'HOORAY!'

The first event was Ivanna's
favourite – the shot put.

What you had to do was hold a ball, twirl around in a circle for a moment or two, then hurl it as far as you could across the lawn. Sir Bobblysock thought it would make a terrible mess of the grass, but he didn't say anything.

Claude watched Ivanna and the other competitors throw the little ball through the air.

'Now it's your turn, Claude!' said
Ivanna, and she handed the ball
to Claude.

It was terribly heavy. Claude
could hardly hold it. But he
tried his best and soon got in the
swing of twirling about in a circle.

Round and round and round
he went.

Sir Bobblysock had one of his funny turns just watching him.

Then FLING! Claude let go of the ball and…

'OUC

...dropped it on Ivanna's toe!

Needless to say, their team did not win this competition.

52

'Don't worry!' groaned Ivanna, clutching her foot. 'Shot put is a bit tricky. Let's see how you do at running…'

The running competition was held on the big oval with the stripes painted on it.

Claude lined up with the other competitors. They seemed a jolly lot – even the two at the end of the line in the striped outfits and masks.

55

'When you hear a bang,' said Ivanna's team mate Reginald Hoofit, 'run as fast as you possibly can!'

Sir Bobblysock thought that it sounded exhausting and was worried Claude might get thirsty on the way round.

Suddenly he had a good idea –
he made Claude pour himself a
nice cup of tea from the flask in
his beret and gave him a few
Garibaldis. He told him to make
sure he had a good slurp of tea
and a biscuit as he ran to keep
his energy up.

PROFESSOR TRUMP'S
WIND
RELIEF
TABLETS

Mr. Lovelybuns
BAKERY BEST
BUNS in
TOWN

Sir Bobblysock went to stand on the side with his earmuffs on as he didn't like loud bangs or the noise of squeaky plimsolls.

Claude got ready.

Claude got steady.

And when the bang went BANG!
Claude and all the other
competitors set off.

Claude ran as fast as he could.
His ears flew out behind him.
Sir Bobblysock was right – running
WAS thirsty work. Thank
goodness he had this cup of tea...

He dunked a biscuit and took a
slurp and – OOPS! – he found
himself flying through the air
again... He was out of control!
His tea and biscuits went
everywhere!

'WATCH OUT!' he cried through a mouthful of biscuit, but it was too late. He landed with a crash on Reginald and they went bouncing off the track and into the crowd.

CRASH

62

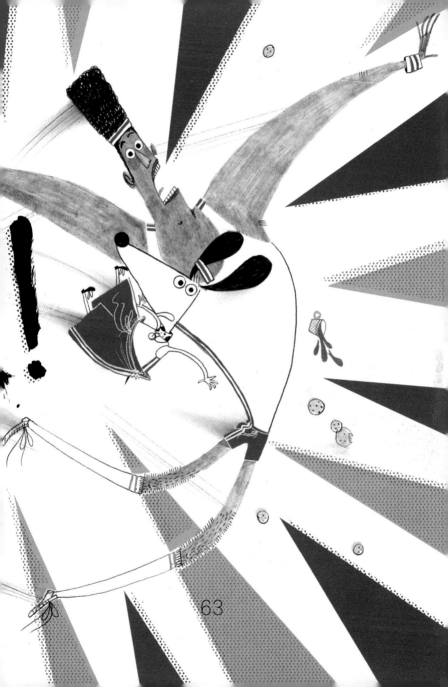

63

'Don't worry,' said Reginald a few minutes later as Ivanna put his arm in a sling, 'you might be better at something else…'

Sadly, that didn't seem to be the case.

Claude tried his best, but nothing seemed to go right…

He and Sir Bobblysock spent so much time blowing up his armbands that Claude missed the swimming competition entirely.

Then, he did a lovely gymnastics routine, but when it came to the bit where he had to waft some ribbons about, Claude got them tangled around his ears AND around the chain of Sir Bobblysock's spectacles, and they both went CRASH! BANG! WALLOP! straight into the judges' table.

It was just disaster…
    after disaster…

It turned out, however, that Sir Bobblysock was quite accomplished at synchronised swimming,

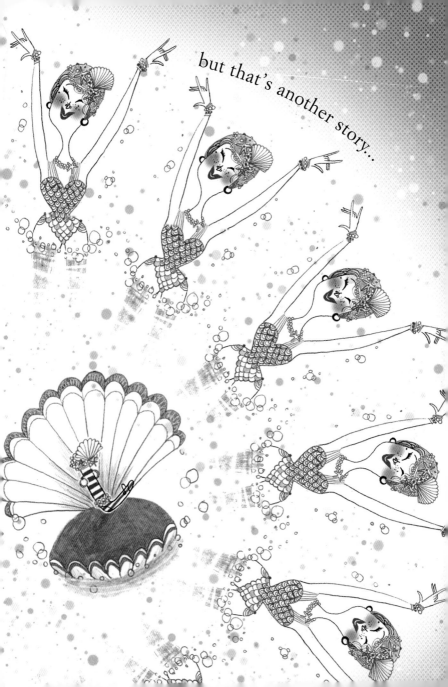

but that's another story...

'Never mind,' said Ivanna a bit sadly when everyone was taking a break, 'maybe we'll do better next year. And there's still the final event.'

Claude sat down next to Sir Bobblysock and swung his legs for a bit. Maybe he shouldn't join in the final event, he thought. Perhaps his team would do better without him. Maybe they'd even win some of those nice shiny medals.

Whilst Claude was thinking this,
Sir Bobblysock was slathering
himself in suncream and having a
good nosy about the stadium.

All of a sudden he jumped!

'What is it, Sir Bobblysock?' said
Claude. He followed Sir
Bobblysock's gaze, and he was
jolly glad he did too!

As he watched, the two people he'd spotted in striped outfits and masks earlier tiptoed sideways like crabs up to the podium with the trophy and medals on it. As quick as a wink, they grabbed them all and slung them into a useful sack that they'd had hidden all day down the leg of their sports knickers!

Sir Bobblysock had ALWAYS had a bad feeling about them.

'STOP!' cried Claude in his loudest Outdoor Voice, and started to run over to them. Sir Bobblysock quickly stashed his suncream into his gentleman's purse and followed. He didn't want to miss out on any of the action.

'WHAT ON EARTH DO YOU THINK YOU ARE DOING?'

cried Claude.

But the naughty robbers didn't stop to answer him – they scarpered!

And at exactly that moment the starting pistol went BANG! and the final event began!

Claude gave chase! Around the track he went, weaving in and out of the other runners. One of the other competitors (a very nice young man) picked Sir Bobblysock up so he could get a better view.

74

Claude chased them into the
cycling arena.

Claude stopped and rummaged
around his beret in his vest.

'Great blundering bone baguettes!'
he cried. He'd left his bike at home
today – just when he needed it!

With an eye on the now cycling robbers, Claude had another rummage around in his beret, found ONE of his roller skates and strapped it on.

WHOOO

SH!

Around
and around the
arena he went,
always almost, but not
quite, catching the crooks…
Then all of a sudden it was off the
bike and onto the trampolines!

Then into the pool house – for the
diving competition!

Claude waited patiently on the ladder for his turn behind the competitors and the thieves. He couldn't quite reach them!

'HAHAHA!' cried the crooks as they jumped off the high board. 'You'll never catch us!'

Claude clattered along the board on his roller-skate and peered over the edge.

Ooh! It was ever so high!

Sir Bobblysock, who was now standing with the lifeguard, started to tremble.

Claude gulped. If he didn't jump, the robbers would get away!

Then he had an idea! Claude gave chase...

He **clanged** through the fencing hall,

hoofed it around the horse racing…

and…

ping-ponged through some *very* tense table tennis matches.

But it was no good – he just couldn't catch up with the robbers. If they made it around the track once more they'd be able to run out of the stadium and escape with the trophy and medals!

Claude needed to beat them to the finish line! But how?

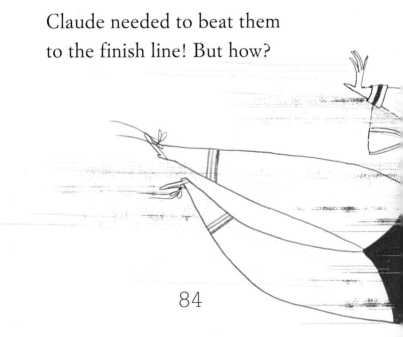

Then Sir Bobblysock had the most wonderful idea. He tooted his whistle and told Ivanna all about it.

She rushed over to the racing Claude and untied his shoelaces with a flourish. Claude immediately tripped over them, just like earlier when he'd hurtled down Waggy Avenue!

Claude flew through the
air and landed straight
on top of the thieves!

The crowd went wild!

Ivanna, Reginald, Sir Bobblysock
and all the other competitors
hurried over to Claude.

'WELL DONE, CLAUDE AND
SIR BOBBLYSOCK!' cried
Ivanna. 'You caught these crooks,
saved the trophy and medals AND
won the final competition!'

The crowd whooped and hollered.
Sir Bobblysock went quite dizzy
with pride.

'Won't you stay and be a world famous sports superstar?' said Ivanna over the noise.

Claude thought about it for a moment. He'd had terrific fun having a go at all the sports, and he looked really quite dashing in his sports kit. But then he also really liked his nice cosy home on Waggy Avenue too.

He explained all this to Ivanna, and also that Sir Bobblysock needed to get back home so he could have a nice lie-down and sort out his hair which was going limp from all the excitement.

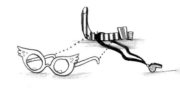

Ivanna said she understood and then proudly presented Claude with his special gold medals and the huge, glitzy trophy. The stadium went WILD!

Then everyone paraded Claude and Sir Bobblysock home, accompanied by the band who played quite a jazzy medley.

Later on, when Mr and Mrs Shinyshoes came home, they were surprised to find a gigantic pair of sports knickers drip-drying on the radiator, and Claude tucked up in bed clutching an enormous trophy.

'Where on earth did it come from?' asked Mrs Shinyshoes. 'Do you think Claude knows something about this?'

Mr Shinyshoes chuckled. 'Of course not!' he laughed. 'He's been asleep here all day!'

But Claude DID know something
about it, and we do too, don't we?

'The author is a comparative newcomer to children's books; on this evidence, he should go far.'

'A handsome creation.'

'Perfect for newly developing readers and great to share.'

'Watch out for this new kid on the children's books block, you will be won over!'

'I loved everything about this book.'